Dear Parent:

Congratulations! Your child is taking the first steps on an exciting journey. The destination? Independent reading!

STEP INTO READING® will help your child get there. The program offers five steps to reading success. Each step includes fun stories and colorful art. There are also Step into Reading Sticker Books, Step into Reading Math Readers, Step into Reading Phonics Readers, Step into Reading Write-In Readers, and Step into Reading Phonics Boxed Sets—a complete literacy program with something for every child.

Learning to Read, Step by Step!

Ready to Read   Preschool–Kindergarten
• big type and easy words • rhyme and rhythm • picture clues
For children who know the alphabet and are eager to begin reading.

Reading with Help   Preschool–Grade 1
• basic vocabulary • short sentences • simple stories
For children who recognize familiar words and sound out new words with help.

Reading on Your Own   Grades 1–3
• engaging characters • easy-to-follow plots • popular topics
For children who are ready to read on their own.

Reading Paragraphs   Grades 2–3
• challenging vocabulary • short paragraphs • exciting stories
For newly independent readers who read simple sentences with confidence.

Ready for Chapters   Grades 2–4
• chapters • longer paragraphs • full-color art
For children who want to take the plunge into chapter books but still like colorful pictures.

STEP INTO READING® is designed to give every child a successful reading experience. The grade levels are only guides. Children can progress through the steps at their own speed, developing confidence in their reading, no matter what their grade.

Remember, a lifetime love of reading starts with a single step!

© 2014 Rainbow S.r.l. and Viacom International Inc. All rights reserved. Published in the United States by Random House Children's Books, a division of Random House LLC, a Penguin Random House Company, 1745 Broadway, New York, NY 10019, and in Canada by Random House of Canada Limited, Toronto. Winx Club and all related characters are trademarks of Rainbow S.r.l. Created by Iginio Straffi. Nickelodeon and all related titles and logos are trademarks of Viacom International Inc.

Step into Reading, Random House, and the Random House colophon are registered trademarks of Random House LLC.

Visit us on the Web!
StepIntoReading.com
randomhouse.com/kids

Educators and librarians, for a variety of teaching tools, visit us at RHTeachersLibrarians.com

ISBN 978-0-385-37489-7 (trade) — ISBN 978-0-385-37490-3 (lib. bdg.)
Printed in the United States of America
10 9 8 7 6 5 4 3 2 1

nickelodeon

Winx CLUB

Dragon Quest

Adapted by Mary Tillworth
Based on the teleplay "Dragon Quest" by Jonathan Foss
Illustrated by Cartobaleno

Random House 🏠 New York

One day,
Bloom visits
an island.
She is on a quest.

She is looking for
her inner dragon.

She needs to find
the Dragon Flame
that lives inside her.

Bloom looks
for a dragon
to help her.

She sees a dragon.

But he is mean!

The dragon opens

his mouth.

<u>Roar!</u>

The dragon swoops
toward Bloom!
The brave fairy
throws a fireball
at the dragon.

The fireball works!
The dragon drops
to the ground.

Three more dragons rise
into the air.
They attack Bloom!

There are
too many dragons!
Bloom runs away.
One dragon breathes fire
at her.

Bloom slips.

She falls into a pit!

In the pit,
Bloom meets
a little dragon.
His name is Buddy.
He is lost.

Bloom tells Buddy
she will help him
get home.

Buddy's home is
on Fire Mountain.
They walk there together.
Bloom tells Buddy
she is sad.

She does not know
how to beat
the mean dragons.

Buddy tells Bloom,
"To beat a dragon,
you must <u>be</u>
a dragon."

Buddy teaches Bloom

how to walk

like a dragon.

Stomp, stomp, stomp!

Buddy shows Bloom
how to eat
like a dragon.

Bloom picks
dragon berries
from the thorny bushes.
Yum, yum!

Bloom must roar
like a dragon.
She tries her best.
Roar!

Roaring is hard!

Bloom and Buddy find Fire Mountain.

A big dragon
guards the mountain.
The big dragon
is asleep.

Bloom and Buddy try
to sneak by.
The big dragon wakes up!

The big dragon
swipes his tail
at Bloom.
Bloom leaps
out of the way.

The big dragon
grabs Buddy!
"Help!" cries Buddy.

Bloom takes
a deep breath
and roars!
She releases
the Dragon Flame!

The big dragon
is scared of Bloom!
He lets go of Buddy.

Bloom has found
her inner dragon!

Bloom and Buddy
make a great team!